Bam-Boo

and

I Wish

'Bam-Boo' and 'I Wish'
An original concept by Alice Hemming
© Alice Hemming

Illustrated by Julia Seal

Published by MAVERICK ARTS PUBLISHING LTD
Studio 3A, City Business Centre, 6 Brighton Road,
Horsham, West Sussex, RH13 5BB
© Maverick Arts Publishing Limited May 2017
+44 (0)1403 256941

A CIP catalogue record for this book is available at the British Library.

ISBN 978-1-84886-251-7

Coventry City Council	
FML	
3 8002 02339 945 6	
Askews & Holts	Jun-2017
BEGINNER READER	£5.99

Maverick
arts publishing
www.maverickbooks.co.uk

This book is rated as: Red Band (Guided Reading)
This story is decodable at Letters and Sounds Phase 2.

Bam-Boo
and
I Wish

By **Alice Hemming**
Illustrated by **Julia Seal**

The Letter B

Trace the lower and upper case letter with a finger. Sound out the letter.

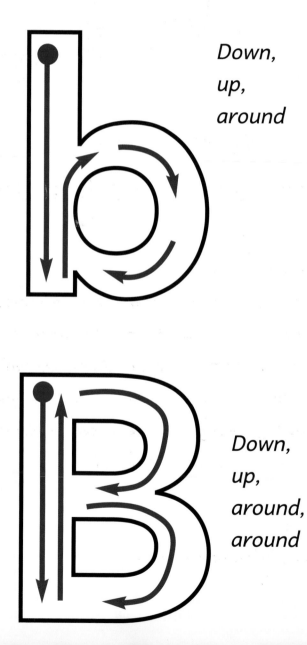

*Down,
up,
around*

*Down,
up,
around,
around*

tree   bird   frog

High-frequency words:

to be you the no it is off has

Tips for Reading 'Bam-Boo'

- Practise the tricky words listed above before reading the story.

- If the reader struggles with any of the other words, ask them to look for sounds they know in the word. Encourage them to sound out the words and help them read the words if necessary.

- After reading the story, ask the reader the places that Bam did not hide and then ask where he did hide.

Fun Activity

Play a game of hide and seek.

Bam is a panda.

Bam has run off!

Can you spot Bam up in the tree?

No, that thing in the tree is a bird.

Can you spot Bam on
the big rocks?

No, a frog is up on the rocks.

Can you spot him in the bam...
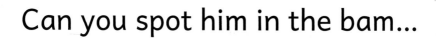

Bam is in the bamboo.

The Letter W

Trace the lower and upper case letter with a finger. Sound out the letter.

Down,

up,

down,

up

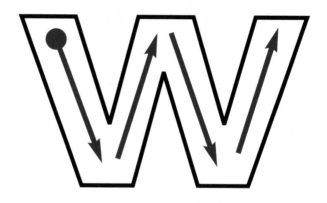

Down,

up,

down,

up

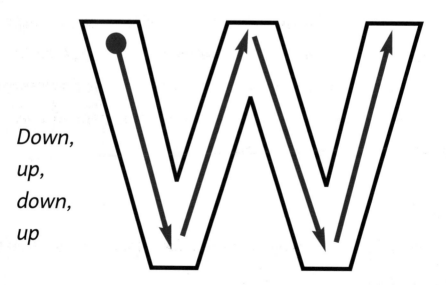

Some words to familiarise:

coin   prince   horse

High-frequency words:

I   the   on   a   in   to

Tips for Reading 'I Wish'

- *Practise the tricky words listed above before reading the story.*
- *If the reader struggles with any of the other words, ask them to look for sounds they know in the word. Encourage them to sound out the words and help them read the words if necessary.*
- *After reading the story, ask the reader if they remember what the different characters wished for.*

Fun Activity

Ask the reader what they would wish for if they went to a magic wishing well.

I Wish

I am the Wishing Well on the hill.
Put a coin in the bucket.

Put a coin in the bucket. Tell me your wish.

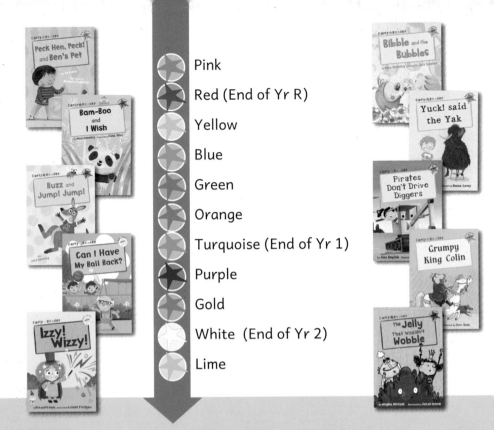

Pink

Red (End of Yr R)

Yellow

Blue

Green

Orange

Turquoise (End of Yr 1)

Purple

Gold

White (End of Yr 2)

Lime

Book Bands for Guided Reading

The Institute of Education book banding system is made up of twelve colours, which reflect the level of reading difficulty. The bands are assigned by taking into account the content, the language style, the layout and phonics.

Children learn at different speeds but the colour chart shows the levels of progression with the national expectation shown in brackets. To learn more visit the IoE website: www.ioe.ac.uk.

All of these books have been book banded for guided reading to the industry standard and edited by a leading educational consultant.

For more titles visit: www.maverickbooks.co.uk/early-readers